The Cruelty of the Fisher King:
A Tale of Perceval and the Grail

by

BARAK A. BASSMAN

TELEMACHUS PRESS

**THE CRUELTY OF THE FISHER KING:
A TALE OF PERCEVAL AND THE GRAIL**

Cover design by Telemachus Press, LLC

Cover art:
Public Domain: Perceval-arrives-at-grail-castle-bnf-fr-12577

Publishing Services by Telemachus Press, LLC
7652 Sawmill Road
Suite 304
Dublin, Ohio 43016
http://www.telemachuspress.com

ISBN: 978-1-956867-37-4 (eBook)
ISBN: 978-1-956867-38-1 (Paperback)

Library of Congress Control Number: 2022912549

Version 2022.07.05

Table of Contents

The Cruelty of the Fisher King:

A Tale of Perceval and the Grail

I. In the Waste Land

FOR MANY WEEKS, Perceval had been riding serenely through the rich lands of the Kingdom of Logres. Although in search of perilous adventures, he had mostly found lush meadows, peaceful forests, and the brightly lit halls of the merry and fat old lords in the castles of the countryside, who were always eager to extend their hospitality to such a famous knight of King Arthur's court. But as he rode along on this road and that, not paying careful attention to where he was going, Perceval stumbled, by accident, into a very different sort of place.

In this land, there were no trees or bushes or grasses, no game roaming about, not even a bird in the air. The dusty ground was strewn with large brownish-red rocks, from whose pores thick, nauseating fumes wafted up, as if the insides of the stones were on fire. Perceval was forced to remove his helmet and gasp for breath. He vomited over the side of his horse, and then a hot, dry wind blew waves of dust into his eyes and mouth. Perceval anxiously looked around for a road leading away from this barren waste, but he saw no way out.

And so, perceiving no better option, he continued to ride forward. As the dark grey clouds above him turned pink at their edges from the setting sun, and his stomach twisted violently with hunger, he wondered if he would be forced to spend the night lying down on the hard ground amongst the rocks, inhaling their poisonous smoke as he tried to sleep.

But then he had a stroke of luck. As Perceval rounded the side of a hill, he suddenly saw a large lake in which he spied a small, but elegant boat holding two men. One stood at the prow with a long oar to steer the ship. He was young and broad-shouldered with a sword hanging loosely from his belt. He wore a scarlet mantle fashioned from what appeared to be expensive fabrics.

The other man was older, but not yet wrinkled with extreme age. He wore an even finer mantle, with an ermine collar. He lay flat on his back, with his head slightly propped up by some object that Perceval could not clearly see. In his hands he held a fishing rod. That gave Perceval a bit of hope—if there were fish in this lake, then maybe he could catch something for his dinner.

Perceval called out a friendly greeting in the name of His Lord and Savior Jesus Christ and King Arthur of Logres.

The young man standing on the prow turned his face toward Perceval and returned the greeting politely, but without any warmth.

What land is this? Perceval asked.

But they did not respond.

Perceval wondered if they had heard him. Or maybe they were embarrassed by this desolate wasteland? Plainly, these were men of high birth and must have their estates nearby. Maybe they thought his question was a cruel attempt to mock the poverty of their domains, and they were shamed into silence. Perceval cursed himself for his foolish tongue.

Still, these noblemen must have some castle or manor, however modest, within an easy ride—especially if they were still loitering in this lake at sunset—and so perhaps they could extend their hospitality to him for the night. That would right his earlier blunder: Perceval could show them due honor by seeking to be their guest.

He called out to the men on the boat again: My Lords, I am a stranger in these lands and far from my home. Do you know where I can find lodging for the night?

Now the older man, the fisherman, still lying flat on his back, spoke: The only place you can reach before the sun sets is the Castle Corbenic. Take that path up the crag—and he pointed to a narrow and steep road wending up the side of a tall hill looming over one side of the lake—and go round to the other side. Just past the hill, a quarter of an hour's ride at the most, you may be fortunate enough to find the Castle Corbenic, where you shall be honorably received and well cared for. Be warned, though: Some men find it; but some do not. However, there is nowhere else close by, so you are best advised to try your luck.

Perceval was baffled. How could there be a fortress just over and past that hill? Surely, he would have already seen the tops of the towers in the distance. And how could some travelers fail to find a castle?

But the fisherman was right: He seemed to have no other option for the night. With the sun fading fast now, and darkness creeping over the rocky ground, Perceval thanked the men on the boat for their good counsel and rode off toward the steep path up the crag.

While a bit difficult to make out in the gloom of the dusk, Perceval was able to follow the road as it snaked across and around the side of the hill and then back down again to level ground.

But he still could not see a castle anywhere.

With his heart sinking, Perceval rode aimlessly forward, his eyes resting on the scattered rocks on the ground. But then, after riding for about a quarter of an hour, he suddenly heard a voice call out loudly: Good Sir! Please halt your horse so we can lower the drawbridge and welcome you properly for the night.

Perceval now looked up. In front of him was a deep trench filled with muddy water and jagged rocks, and across the trench were high stone walls and soaring towers. He could not understand how he had failed to notice such an immense fortress looming before him. Perhaps the putrid fumes from the boulders had dulled his senses, or maybe it was the hunger.

The drawbridge was quickly lowered over the moat, and three well-dressed young men ran over to Perceval, helped him down from the saddle, and took his horse by the bridle. Once they were inside the castle walls, his charger was led away to the stables. The young men disarmed Perceval and dressed him in a soft mantle.

Following these same young men into the hall, Perceval was astounded by the luxury of the palace. Gone was the nauseating stench of the smoke rising from the rocks; Perceval now smelled only cinnamon and clove. The stones in the walls were thick and perfectly hewn, and there were bright, long tapers to light the way. Huge, colorful tapestries hung in the hall, which depicted scenes in a lush forest where a strikingly beautiful woman of pale complexion presided over a kingdom of serene and peaceful wild animals.

Perceval was seated on a couch and served sweet wine, freshly baked bread, and a round of soft cheese. The young men said that dinner would commence shortly, told him to call out if he should need anything in the meantime, and then disappeared out of the hall into a side corridor.

Perceval dug greedily into his food and drink. Everything was superb. He wondered how such delicacies could have been acquired in such a miserable, impoverished land—after all, what could a fat cow eat amidst these rocks? And where could the grapes have grown or the wheat been harvested?

After a time, a large group of elegantly dressed men of various ages entered the great hall and sat themselves down on the couches spread about the room. They offered friendly, albeit brief, greetings to Perceval, and he responded in kind. And then they fell to talking amongst themselves. No one asked Perceval for his name, much less from whence he hailed or how he had wound up a guest in their castle.

Perceval considered asking one of these men to explain the strange marvels he had seen—both the marvel of the desolate, choking wasteland and the marvel of the seemingly hidden castle overflowing with sumptuous comforts and delights. But then he recalled how ashamed the men on the boat had been when he had asked them about these lands. Better not to ask questions that could embarrass his hosts, he reminded himself. In time, his thoughts continued, as the wine flows tonight, tongues will loosen and the secret of these wonders will be revealed. For now, he would rest his aching bones and relax in silence.

Comforted by these reflections, Perceval drank again from his goblet, which had just been discreetly refilled.

After a while, four sturdy, handsome young men entered the hall carrying a litter, in the middle of which lay the elegantly dressed fisherman from the lake, once again flat on his back and apparently unable to move his body. They made their way to where Perceval was sitting and carefully lowered their burden down onto the floor in front of him. Then they each grabbed a leg or an arm and gently hoisted the fisherman onto a couch next to Perceval, before lifting up again the now empty litter and exiting from the hall.

Perceval greeted him and praised the hall for its wealth and beauty.

The fisherman smiled contentedly. He said that he was the lord of this castle and always delighted to host a knight errant who had wandered far and wide in search of bold adventures.

Perceval noted that, once again, the man did not give his name or the name of the kingdom over which he ruled. There had to be some secret that explained the wretched poverty of the land and the suffering of its crippled lord. But as a guest who had been shown only the greatest honor and respect, he reasoned that he should not ask about such undoubtedly shameful matters.

So instead, Perceval turned the conversation toward himself. He said that he had indeed wandered far and wide. He spoke of his childhood in Wales with his mother, a noble widow who had shunned the world in her grief after her husband was slain in battle. Avoiding her ancestors' castle, she had chosen to raise her son in the peaceful but solitary glades of an immense forest. He told how, as a young man, he had hunted boars and stags with crudely fashioned wooden spears.

The lord of the castle sighed wistfully and said that he too recalled once, long ago, riding through thick woods and stalking fierce and quick beasts.

Perceval then recounted how he had put his spear-throwing skills to use for his lord King Arthur. When he had first come to the royal court at Camelot, there was an uproar because a haughty knight in vermillion armor had brazenly laid claim to huge swaths of Arthur's domains. As proof that he did not fear the king or recognize his rights, this rogue stole a golden cup from the palace. Perceval, who was not even a squire then, encountered this traitor in the meadows just beyond the walls of Camelot and felled him with one fast throw of a spear straight through his eyes and out the back of his skull. The wretch had instantly tumbled to the ground dead. As a reward for his boldness, King Arthur made Perceval a knight and gifted him the dead traitor's vermillion arms and powerful horse.

The lord of the castle praised Perceval for his courage in challenging a knight so much more experienced and skilled than he had been at the time. This recalled to mind, he continued, a tale he had once heard of another haughty knight. But before he could start this tale, the lord of the castle suddenly fell silent—as did all the other men in the hall.

At first, Perceval was confused, but then he saw, from a distant corner in the hall, a procession of five women. They were tall and lithe and clad in identical white gowns and thick veils. Perceval would not have been able to tell one from the other. Two women walked in front, side by side, holding long white tapers. They were followed by a woman holding what looked like a wide, oval-shaped golden bowl or dish of some kind. And behind her were the last two maidens, also walking side by side and holding long white tapers.

None of the women spoke and no one greeted them.

The procession wound its way slowly across the hall until the maidens approached the lord of the castle lying flat on his couch. As they came nearer, Perceval was overwhelmed with the most wonderful smells—fruits and flowers, spices and herbs and incense, as if all the world's loveliest scents were rising forth at the very same time from the dish the maiden carried.

When they reached the crippled lord, the four maidens holding tapers retreated behind the maiden holding the dish. Meanwhile, the maiden holding the dish walked over to her lord, knelt down, and held the dish up to his lips.

Perceval was now able to get a closer look at this dish. Its gold glowed brilliantly and the craftsmanship was extraordinary. Its edges were decorated with finely wrought, almost disturbingly realistic, miniature figures of men with curly hair and beards and goats' feet and horns, who were playing pipes and flutes. There was something lecherous and mischievous in their eyes. Perceval shuddered at the sight of these demonic rogues and turned his gaze back to the smooth, unadorned center of the dish.

The dish was empty at first. But then foods suddenly appeared, meats, cheeses, vegetables, fruits, pastries, before, just as suddenly, they vanished into the air. Each time a new delicacy was revealed, Perceval heard a soft, barely audible music, as if the tiny pipes and flutes the little golden goat-men were holding in their arms were being played.

The lord of the castle did not try to eat any of these foods. Nor did he speak. Rather, he lifted the maiden's veil and stroked her red hair and her cheeks. Her face was deathly pale and finely chiseled, as if the same smith who had made the goat-men from gold had fashioned her from ivory. She frowned at the liberties being taken with her body, but she did not resist him.

After a few minutes, he closed the maiden's veil again and withdrew his hand. She rose with her dish, the four other maidens resumed their original places, and their procession went back the way they had come, mutely but unhurriedly exiting from the hall.

Once the maidens had left, the men in the hall resumed speaking to one another just as they had before, as if nothing had happened.

But the lord of the castle was silent. He looked at Perceval, and his eyes seemed full of sadness and pain. A tear slowly tumbled down his cheek.

Perceval was not sure what to do. He wished to know the meaning of the procession of maidens and the extraordinary dish and why his noble host was now so overwhelmed by despair. But then he checked himself: If the lord of the castle wished to speak of his sorrow, then he would do so. His silence no doubt meant that there was some shameful secret, which it would be wrong to press him to reveal.

As these thoughts ran through Perceval's mind, the four handsome, sturdy youths reappeared with their litter, raised their lord back up onto it, and carried him from the hall.

Perceval bade his host a good night and thanked him again for his hospitality.

But the lord of the castle did not answer.

Then the other men in the hall also rose and walked away, leaving Perceval alone and unsure what to do. Fortunately, one of the servants who had carried the litter returned and showed Perceval to his room.

He passed a blissful night in a soft, decadent bed. Indeed, he slept so well, that when he finally opened his eyes again, it was clearly well past the hour of prime. After yawning and stretching and stumbling back into his clothes, he left his room and went into the corridor hoping to find a servant who could lead him back to the lord of the castle.

But he saw no one.

Perplexed again, Perceval wandered throughout the palace, but in every room and hallway he found himself alone in the eerie quiet. Eventually he went down into the castle courtyard, where he found his arms and his horse set out for him. Perceval put his arms back on and mounted his charger, thinking that, perhaps, he would ride out from the castle gates and go find his host fishing again in his boat on the lake.

But after riding across the lowered drawbridge, he suddenly heard sharp hissing sounds, as if a thousand snakes were ready to pounce upon his flesh. He turned around and saw that the drawbridge had been raised. He called out to the ramparts, assuming that somebody had to be there, but there was no response.

II. The Loathly Lady

PERCEVAL EVENTUALLY FOUND his way out of the wasteland and back to the lush forests of Logres. Soon the path he was following opened onto a wide meadow, where—much to his happy surprise—he found that King Arthur and his court had pitched their tents. Arthur warmly greeted Perceval and ordered that an additional pavilion be erected for his use.

Under a bright sun and a cloudless blue sky, Perceval passed several pleasant days hunting, sparring, and feasting. After so many months of solitary wandering, he welcomed the chance to rejoin the company of the other knights of the Round Table. They laughed together and jested at one another's expense, and argued heatedly about which of the noble ladies in Queen Guinevere's household was the loveliest.

And they traded tales of their adventures—of giants and dragons, of robbers and cutthroats, and of castles with perilous beds where you would be shot full of arrows the moment you lay down. Sir Gawain even recounted how, after barely surviving the volley of arrows on the dangerous bed, he had been attacked by a lion, which an evil sorcerer had set as a guard over the noble ladies held captive in his castle. Lingering with relish over each detail of the fight, Gawain regaled the other knights with the story of how he had battled and felled the vicious beast; he proudly showed off the severed lion's claw still stuck to his shield.

Perceval, too, recounted his adventures. He described how he had slaughtered a gang of highway robbers who had been terrorizing merchants and travelers on the king's roads. He had bested a wicked knight in single combat, and made the man swear to end his cruel mistreatment of his wife, whom he had falsely charged with adultery. He had even fought a giant serpent, although there had been no clear victor in that struggle.

But Perceval decided not to speak of the wasteland and the Castle Corbenic. He was not sure what to say—the adventure had been so strange. And he felt, somehow, that he had acted dishonorably. He recalled how the crippled lord of the castle, the fisherman from the lake, had looked at him with such anguish in his eyes. And that next morning, when he had been left alone and then hissed at as he departed, he felt as if he was being punished for some unnamed yet terrible offense by banishment from the luxurious delights of that marvelously rich hall. What could he say to Gawain and Kay and Sagremore about all of this? There was no victory over anyone or anything, or even a battle. There was only a vague, haunting sense that Perceval had failed to do something that had been expected of him but he did not know what that thing was. He resolved to put this baffling episode out of his mind and be grateful to God that he had safely returned from a land of cursed and bizarre enchantments back to the light of day in the good Christian realm of Logres.

It was a beautiful moonlit evening in King Arthur's camp, the air was warm but not heavy, and the fireflies glowed in the dark blue of the spreading evening. Perceval and his fellow knights were seated with their king around a circular table inside a wide pavilion, feasting merrily on the succulent meat of the boars that they had felled in the morning's hunt. Queen Guinevere was the only woman there, gently teasing each knight about his particular lady love—and drawing out more than a few blushes and stammers.

Perceval smiled peacefully as he slowly drank down yet another tall goblet of mead.

But then a stranger burst into the tent. Alarmed, the knights instinctively jumped to their feet and drew their swords. Yet when they saw that the intruder was a bent old woman standing there alone, they sat down again and put away their weapons. As she walked towards the light spread by the tapers in the pavilion, Perceval shuddered in horror: Her head was bald, except for a few stray strands of hair that resembled strings from a spider's web; her black eyes were unnaturally large, practically bulging out of their sockets; her jaw jutted too far forward with huge, crooked teeth peeking out like sharp jagged rocks. And there were moist, hairy moles all over her cheeks and lips.

Then there was her stench: It was as if a heap of venison meat had suddenly gone rancid.

Rendering her appearance even stranger, her hideous form was dressed in an elegant silk gown of clearly exceptional tailoring. Her shoes were also of fine and expensive make and not worn down in the slightest, leading Perceval to conclude that she must have ridden, not walked, to King Arthur's camp. Her fingers, too, were long, delicate, and refined—not a callus in sight—and so this was obviously not a lowborn woman who labored with her hands.

But why, Perceval wondered to himself, would a noble lady travel alone, not be announced, and take such poor care of her appearance? Wouldn't a highborn woman, in her age and condition, use strong perfumes and thick veils to artfully conceal her ugliness?

King Arthur hailed the strange old woman with a friendly greeting: My Lady, I bid you most welcome in the name of Our Lord Jesus Christ and His Holy Virgin Mother. Come, sit by my wife Guinevere and share in our feast. You have my sincere apologies that you were not properly announced. Please tell me if you need a horse tended or servants provided with food and drink. After you have eaten and regained your strength—for you must have been journeying some ways to reach this meadow—then you can tell us your name and from whence you come. Now, come, sit down and join us. Any good Christian lady is always welcome at my table.

But the ugly old woman replied harshly: King Arthur, stop wasting your fine words. I will never sit down to eat with men as vile as you and your knights. You are all a blight upon this once great land of Britain. How can you feast and make merry when the evidence of your terrible crimes is right before you, glaring and obvious to anyone with eyes to see?

Perceval felt his blood boil at these words. If this were a man, his sword would already have been on the bastard's throat. But he restrained himself: This is an old woman wandering about the woods. Her reason must have grown feeble with age.

King Arthur answered her, his voice calm and gentle: My Lady, I fear you have misjudged us. We are not criminals or traitors here. Accept our hospitality and let us show you what good Christians we are in Logres. If any wicked men have rightly incurred your wrath, whoever and wherever they may be, I will send my knights to hunt them down and bring them to justice.

The hideous crone now emitted a hissing sound—the very same sound Perceval had heard coming down from the ramparts of the Castle Corbenic when he rode off across the drawbridge. Then, in a voice quivering with anger, she spoke again: Do not address me as if I was a doddering old imbecile. I know who you are, and I know what you are, and I can see through the illusions of piety and virtue that you try to weave about your pitiful, putrid realm. You are the lord of traitors and cowards. You permit a foul and unrepentant criminal to share your feast tonight—in this tent and at this moment. If you were as honorable as you pretend to be, you would have long ago cast him out. His presence alone is enough to damn you and all your lies.

Arthur now sat bolt upright and leaned slightly forward. With a new firmness in his voice, he demanded that the woman stop speaking in riddles. If she wished to lodge an accusation against a knight seated there in his tent, then she should speak plainly and state her grievance. Otherwise, she would no longer be welcome to remain in his camp.

She smirked and answered in a voice that was both unsettlingly calm and brimming with spite: I most certainly can satisfy your wish, little king. The criminal is there—and she pointed to Perceval.

And of what crime, King Arthur responded, do you accuse Sir Perceval?

The greatest crime I can imagine, little king, the crime of a cruelty without equal. Sir Perceval had the opportunity to save a noble lord, a good man, from endless, horrible suffering and to restore prosperity to his ravaged land. He only needed to utter a few words. But this pitiless knight, your Sir Perceval, with a stone in his breast where his heart should be, lacked the compassion to act. That was his crime.

I see from your faces that your fine and noble friend Sir Perceval has not yet regaled you with the tale of his adventure at the Castle Corbenic, where he enjoyed the bountiful hospitality of its lord, the good Fisher King. The Fisher King once reigned over a rich and lush land. But then he was treacherously wounded between his upper thighs. This blow should have killed him, but his faithful liegemen brought him back in time to his palace, where the enchantment of the magic grail, the wondrous golden dish from which the lords of Corbenic are served, was able to sustain his life.

But this life is like a death: He cannot walk or ride or even sit up. And while the grail's sorcery can prevent his death, his wound cannot heal. His only solace is to lie down in a boat in his fairest lake and cast out his fishing rod.

With its lord and master no longer fully a man, the land withered. The wheat and the fruit trees and the vines withered away.

The game fled to other pastures. His peasants, too, all died or fled. The once bountiful domain became a wasteland of hot wind, dust, and jagged rocks. Yet the grail's magic has protected the Castle Corbenic. Within its walls, luxury and wealth befitting the high birth of the Fisher King still remain.

But Sir Perceval could have healed the Fisher King's wound and redeemed the land. He had wandered into the wasteland and spent the night as a guest at Corbenic, where the Fisher King sat Perceval in a place of honor by his side at a sumptuous banquet. During this meal, the maidens who safeguard the grail brought it before their lord. At that moment, if Perceval had only asked a simple question—Whom does the grail serve?—then the wound would have healed, and the land would have blossomed and prospered once again.

But in his cruelty, Sir Perceval said nothing. After the grail maidens left the hall, the Fisher King stared in silence at Perceval, with such anguish and longing in his eyes, but Perceval thought only of stuffing his gullet with the exquisite delicacies that the grail's magic brings forth.

In sorrow and shame, the Fisher King and his court fled from Perceval's loathsome presence.

On the following morning, Perceval was banished from the Castle Corbenic and its enchantments and riches.

And then the criminal is welcomed back into your camp. More than merely welcomed—honored, as if he were a model of chivalry and virtue. Hence you can understand why, little king, I accuse you and your lords: You merrily break bread with the foulest, most selfish knight in all of Britain. Perceval's presence here brings shame upon you all.

And with that, the ugly woman stormed out of the pavilion. After a moment of stunned silence, Arthur dispatched a squire to fetch her back. But when the squire returned, he said that she had vanished without a trace.

III. The Shunning

ONCE THE SQUIRE had confirmed that the stranger had disappeared, the knights seated in Arthur's tent fell silent and showed no inclination to resume their feasting and drinking. Queen Guinevere then suggested that His Majesty's brave and noble knights must be quite exhausted from a long day of hunting in the forest and practicing their charges in the meadow—and it had suddenly gotten so dark—perhaps it was time for each man to return to his own tent to rest for the night?

King Arthur immediately agreed, granted them leave to disperse, and wished everyone a good evening.

But Perceval was too stunned by the hideous lady's insults to be able to sleep. He walked off by himself to the edge of the camp, to a small clearing before the forest began. He sat down on the grass and looked up at the sky. The evening was tranquil and warm, without a cloud in sight, and the stars glistened next to the soft white moon. The peaceful night soothed his raging nerves, as if the Earth had indifferently shrugged off the ugly woman's accusations.

And what of those accusations? He was glad to learn, at last, something of the secrets of the Castle Corbenic—of the Fisher King's wound, the curse upon the land, and the magic of the grail. But how could he have known that he was supposed to ask a particular question at a precise moment to heal the Fisher King? If that were the case, why didn't anyone in that castle explain to him what he was tasked to do?

Who was she? Had he met her before? She must have been a denizen of that wretched wasteland. Perceval racked his brain to try to remember every face he had seen in the Castle Corbenic, but the only women he recalled were the five lovely maidens who brought the grail in and out of the great hall—they certainly bore no resemblance to the repulsive crone. Perhaps there were other women servants in the castle? Aged female relations of the Fisher King? He could not be sure.

If the hag was even human. How could a woman that old and decrepit travel such a distance by herself? She would never have had the stamina to ride a palfrey for so many miles. And how would she have eaten? There were long stretches of road with nowhere to seek hospitality for the night. Perceval himself had been forced to sleep on the ground and hunt wild game for his meals. But a feeble old woman like that would not be able to kill her dinner.

Perceval thus concluded that she could not have been a human woman. But then what was she? A demon? A fairy? Some haunted spirit of the old Druid Britain, from the dark time before the truth of the Christian faith had spread its light over these lands? Whatever she was, she was ungodly and cursed—*she* was the evil one, not him.

She had to be a demon, Perceval mused again, and that whole wasteland was a slice of hell. The riches of that palace were clearly an illusion conjured by the Devil's enchantments. Cursed be the whole damn evil adventure.

Feeling calmer now, he stood back up and returned to his pavilion to rest for the night. While he was sure that neither his lord King Arthur nor any of his fellow knights would give any credence to that demon crone's wild ravings—for they too would see clearly that Perceval was being hounded by some infernal, unchristian spirit—nevertheless, he was careful to avoid contact with anyone else on the way back to his tent. The thought of discussing the hag's rantings simply filled him with too much dread and exhaustion.

After Perceval awoke the next morning and dressed, he went out to look for his fellow knights to join them in the morning's hunt. However, seeing no one else about, he cornered one of the servants who looked after the hunting dogs at night; this man told him that King Arthur and the other knights had already left for the hunt without him.

Perceval realized that he must have slept for too long. Although it was strange that no one had tried to wake him.

Still, Perceval tried not to feel slighted. He busied himself looking after his horse, checking with the grooms about the care it had been receiving and making sure it had plenty of oats to eat. Then he looked around the camp for a skilled and agile sparring partner against whom to practice his swordsmanship, but was frustrated to find only pimple-faced, skinny youths who had just been made squires.

Feeling restless, he decided to saddle and mount his charger and make for the nearest chapel. He had not been confessed in many weeks and it would surely be good for his soul to hear a Mass sung. Perhaps the Devil was persecuting him because he had not tended sufficiently to the care of his Christian faith.

Perceval rode briskly across the meadow and down a meandering path into the forest. After three quarters of an hour, he reached a modest grey chapel next to a hermitage, from which arose the faint, but sweet, sounds of holy chanting. He dismounted, tied his horse to a post in front of the hermitage, and quietly entered the little church.

A withered, tiny man in a coarse brown robe far too big for his skeletal frame was kneeling down in front of the altar and singing his prayers. His body trembled. Deeply stirred, Perceval removed his weapons, left them at the door, and advanced toward the altar intending to kneel down and pray too. But as Perceval came close, the holy hermit abruptly stopped his prayers and rose to his feet.

Towering over the old priest, Perceval bent down slightly, in a gesture of respect, and offered greetings in the name of God, the Holy Virgin Mother, and King Arthur.

The hermit returned Perceval's greeting in a thin, gentle voice. He administered the Eucharist to the knight and they prayed together. Perceval then made confession of his sins and received absolution.

However, his confession did not make mention of his adventure at the Castle Corbenic with the Fisher King and the grail. He was determined not to give any credence to the ugly old woman's vile slanders, even here.

By the time Perceval returned to King Arthur's pavilions, it was nearly the hour of nones and the other knights had returned from their hunt. Relieved to see his comrades again, Perceval dismounted and bounded over towards Sagremore, Kay, Bors, and Lionel, who were lounging about together on the thick grass, laughing and drinking wine.

But when Perceval approached them, they fell silent and their faces suddenly glazed over with a grim earnestness, as if they had been abruptly interrupted by a solemn funeral procession.

Perceval tried to be merry: My good knights, what wine are you drinking? Did you ride out to the hunt this morning? Will we feast on fresh boar meat tonight?

Yet they remained silent and turned their eyes to the ground.

Perceval tried again: Did the hunt go so poorly that it would stain your honor to tell about it?

Sagremore now spoke, although he still did not look Perceval in the eye: The hunt went well, thanks and praise to God. We felled two fine boars and a fat stag.

Perceval forced himself to smile and said, with as much gaiety as he could muster: That was certainly a fine morning's hunt. But why didn't you wake me to come along? With my spear by your side, there could have been a third boar for our feast tonight.

But Sagremore did not respond.

After a lengthy pause, Kay looked up and spoke: Sir Perceval, I must apologize for forgetting to rouse you this morning—I was careless in my haste. But we are all tired from the hunt, and need to return to our tents to rest before dinner.

And then the four knights stood up and walked away, each going off in a different direction. Perceval thought about maybe following one of them, trying again to coax some sign of friendship, but then he reasoned that they might truly be exhausted and it was probably best to leave them be.

Still, this encounter had left Perceval feeling uneasy. Hungry for some reassuring word, he wandered about the camp, forcing himself to cry out loud greetings to the knights and the squires. But at the sight of him, they all turned away in silence, as if his face were covered in hideous, bubbling boils.

He reflected that the only cause for him to be suddenly so despised must be the ugly old hag's slanders. But why would these knights, men whom he had known for years, men whom he had fought beside in so many battles and tournaments, believe that crone's wild accusations? It was as if *she* had been their longtime companion and he the stranger.

And the crime he was accused of—not asking a very particular question of his crippled host at a feast? What madness was this? He had always been taught to be careful not to speak, even without ill intent, words that could shame another man. In a strange castle, seated next to a lord who had clearly suffered so much pain and anguish, that is precisely what Perceval had done—took painstaking care not to utter any stray word that could bring shame upon the Fisher King.

If the Fisher King had truly needed for Perceval to ask the question whom the grail serves, then somebody in that bewildering fortress should have told him. There was no way for a stranger from a distant land to know about such an unusual custom. The Fisher King had been attended by many liegemen and servants. Surely, any blame should fall on one of them for having been silent when Perceval entered the Castle Corbenic. A word from one of them—which, to believe the ranting demon hag, would only have been a kindness and mercy to their ailing lord—and Perceval would have known to ask the fateful question at the right time and he would have certainly done so.

Yes, the men of the castle were to blame. And then they dispatched this repulsive crone to ride after Perceval and slander him to deflect from their own guilt. Sending an old woman was very clever: If a man had come and so brazenly accused him, Perceval would have issued a challenge on the spot and vindicated his honor in a trial by combat. But how could a knight challenge a decrepit old woman?

With his despair turning quickly now to rage, Perceval decided to confront his fellow knights of Camelot, or at least one of them. Out of the corner of his eye he spied Gawain walking across the meadow. Although Gawain started to move away as Perceval came near, Perceval ran after him and jumped on Gawain's back, knocking him to the ground. After pinning Gawain down beneath his knees, Perceval demanded to know why he was being treated with such scorn.

Because you have brought shame upon us, Gawain answered.

What shame have I brought upon you?

You heard the old woman's words last night. You failed in your adventure. You let a curse linger upon a wretched land and a crippled lord continue to suffer in agony, and yet all you had to do was to speak a few quick words—ask a simple question—at the appropriate moment.

But Perceval replied, with the frustration vibrating in his voice: *I did nothing shameful.*

To which Gawain answered calmly: Did the lady speak any falsehood? Did you not ride to the wasteland, stay the night with the Fisher King at his castle, and then fail to ask the question?

Perceval admitted that this was all true.

And yet you told no one of this adventure? Gawain continued. Why did we have to learn of it from the old woman? If you did nothing shameful, why didn't *you* tell the tale? You beheld so many marvels—the cursed and arid land, the splendor of the rich castle, the magic grail dish—the kinds of marvels that Our Lord King Arthur longs to hear told. The only explanation for your silence was that you knew that you had acted shamefully and you sought to hide your disgrace from us. It is bad enough to act foully, but you had no contrition in your unfeeling heart. If you had truly felt the remorse that a good Christian should feel when he has wronged another, then you would have told the tale and sought a means for atonement.

But Perceval continued to press his case: What act did I do that was shameful? I was a guest for the night in a strange castle, far away from Logres. What act did I do there that has brought shame upon you and My Lord King Arthur?

Gawain replied again in the same calm tone: But the noble lady told what you did that was shameful: You failed to ask the question—whom does the grail serve?—that would have healed both the land and the Fisher King.

Bursting with rage, Perceval leaned closely into Gawain's placid, smug face pinned beneath him and thundered: But how could I have known that I was to ask *that* question, when no one in the castle told me what had to be done?

Yet Gawain answered coldly: You must have known—there must have been signs—hints. Perhaps you missed them; perhaps that was your sin. Again, if you had not erred in some way, why did you conceal this adventure when you returned to us and we all shared accounts of the battles we had fought and the marvels we had seen? You have conducted yourself like a man who knows he is guilty of a crime.

Seething with such rage that he was no longer able to form words in his throat, Perceval clenched his fist and punched Gawain in the jaw. Gawain, in turn, threw Perceval off of him, although he did not return the blow. Instead, he walked quietly away.

Perceval chose to spend that night alone in an empty tent at the edge of the meadow, sending word that he was feeling ill and could not join the evening's feast. A servant brought him a small pitcher of mead and a few cold, tough cuts of meat.

The next morning, he was summoned to King Arthur's pavilion, for a private audience.

With a sad and disappointed look on his face, Arthur spoke to Perceval: My Lord, Sir Perceval, I have always esteemed you as an honorable Christian and a fine knight. Certainly, the finest knight in Wales. Maybe even the finest in Logres. You have brought fame and wealth to my court. For these boons, I am now, and I will always be, profoundly grateful and humbly in your debt. I have shown you all the honor that was within my power to bestow, and I have refused you nothing.

But unfortunately, certain troubling events have recently come to pass that make it difficult for you to remain here at my side. You have been publicly accused of a terrible crime, of cursing a land and its noble lord to endless suffering out of cruel indifference and a lack of Christian love and mercy. I myself cannot weigh the justness of the accusation. I have held no trial, and I have heard no witnesses properly examined before me. Yet the accusation lingers like a foul odor in the air. As long as you are with me in my pavilions, standing by my side as a knight of this court, men may doubt the honor of the crown of Logres—for what honorable king would shelter and reward an unrepentant criminal?

Thus, to preserve the honor of the kingdom of Logres, you must leave now and put these accusations to rest. Travel back to that wasteland and stride again into the great hall of the Castle Corbenic and this time you shall ask the fateful question. Achieve the adventure and heal the Fisher King's wound. Then you may return, as a great and worthy knight errant—perhaps the greatest and worthiest of them all. But as long as you remain here, your shame, and my shame, and all our shame, will only grow.

Perceval protested his innocence—he could not have known about the question that had to be asked, and it was the Fisher King's liegemen who were the true criminals for not telling him about it.

King Arthur nodded solemnly and sympathetically as Perceval spoke. He agreed that Perceval *could* be wholly innocent and unjustly accused. But such ultimate and infallible justice was only for God in Heaven to mete out in His Infinite and Boundless Wisdom. In this earthly world, cursed and degraded by Adam's original sin, men regrettably take malicious joy in spreading slander and gossip, especially when they can spite famous knights and great lords. There is a peculiar pleasure, Arthur mused, that weaker men feel when the strong are humiliated. And so, a wise and prudent king must recognize that grave accusations, even if false or exaggerated, can bring tumult and danger to his land.

Hence it was best for Perceval to depart. In the end, Arthur assured him, God in His Abundant Goodness and Love always guides us from the path of sin and suffering to the joys of redemption and salvation. You shall return to my court having restored life and bounty to the wasteland and healed the Fisher King of his wound, and no man or woman will ever again be able to speak an ill word against you.

IV. Wandering

THE FOLLOWING MORNING, Perceval rode off alone from King Arthur's camp. He intended to follow the king's counsel and return to the Castle Corbenic to ask the fateful question and end the suffering of the Fisher King and his lands. However, he did not know the path to take back to the wasteland. He had stumbled upon it before by pure chance and had not wanted to return once he had left. And thus, he had made no attempt to remember the roads he had followed. Making matters worse, as far as he knew, no other knight had ever traveled there and could show him the route. So, Perceval resigned himself to wandering, trying as best he could to figure out the way back to the wasteland.

But Perceval was also wary of receiving further slights to his honor. Thus, for several days, he kept to remote forest paths and avoided the company of other men, sleeping under the stars and eating fish he caught in the streams.

But then one afternoon the skies darkened, and, reasoning that a storm was approaching, he left the forest paths to pick up the wide old Roman road. After riding for a couple of hours, he spied a castle in the distance and headed toward it. When he arrived at the ramparts, Perceval shouted to the sentries that he was a Christian knight of King Arthur's court in need of lodging for the evening.

The drawbridge was quickly lowered and two squires hurried out to escort Perceval into the fortress. He was disarmed in the courtyard, his horse was stabled, and he was given a fine mantle to wear and a comfortable room in which to rest before the evening meal.

Dinner was served in the hall. There, Perceval made idle chatter with the young squires, giving them advice on the proper care of horses and how to tell a sturdy sword forged from trustworthy metal from a flimsy one that would shatter to pieces in the heat of battle. He regaled them with his boldest victories in years gone by and took pleasure in seeing their rapt, worshipful eyes fixed upon him.

But then the lord and lady of the castle entered the hall, with a smattering of vassals and priests in tow. As one of the squires stood to introduce Perceval, his lord cut him off and shouted in outrage: You stupid lout, don't you see that this is Sir Perceval? How could you have granted him admission to this castle? Don't you know what shame his presence will bring upon us?

Perceval, silently reminding himself to act with courtesy and chivalry, forced out a reply in a gentle voice: My Lord, I am indeed Sir Perceval and I greet you in the name of our Holy Savior Jesus Christ and His Majesty King Arthur. I came here seeking shelter for the night from the gathering storm. If I have ever wronged you in any way—and I do not recall that we have met before—please tell me and I will grant whatever favor you seek to make amends.

The lord of the castle, however, only frowned more deeply and answered harshly: It is not me whom you have wronged, but that long-suffering crippled lord in the wasteland, the Fisher King. Your heart of stone would not deign to utter a few kind words to heal him—and you dare now to give greetings in the name of Our Lord Jesus Christ, Whose commands to love and be merciful you have so cruelly scorned. If my good Christian friends should hear that I extended my hospitality to you, they would judge me to have approved of your base conduct and would rightly condemn me too. Hence, I order you to depart from my walls at once.

Perceval felt his wrath starting to boil. It was one thing for great knights like Arthur and Gawain to pass judgment on his conduct. But this fat pompous fool whom Arthur had sent to garrison this petty outpost? Who was he to say how a knight of the Round Table should conduct himself?

So, Perceval put his rude host back in his proper place: My Lord, a man should weigh his words carefully. From your big soft belly, I can see that it has been many years since you mounted a charger with a lance in your arm and a shield around your neck—if you ever did so. It is not for men like you to judge what is honorable or not for a knight errant. I have done no wrong to you. I merely seek a place to rest for the night. As a Christian and a vassal of Our Lord King Arthur, you should be grateful for the opportunity to show your worth by extending your hospitality to me. But instead, you greet me with insults and scorn. Should you choose to continue to speak these slanders about me, I will be compelled to challenge you to a trial by combat to vindicate my honor. As my cause is just, God will doubtless ensure that I will prevail.

Perceval then reclined in his chair. Smirking, he watched the castellan's retainers—a gaggle of ageing ladies with over-painted faces, fidgety priests, and willowy men with nervous darting eyes— whisper hurriedly amongst each other. Then the plump lord, with downcast eyes, shuffled quickly out of the hall, without taking his leave or saying another word.

At last, the lady of the castle spoke: Sir Perceval, please forgive my husband his ill temper. He has been afflicted of late with a terrible fever and his reason is clouded. I told him that he was not yet well enough for company, but he was so overjoyed to host a knight errant that he insisted upon coming down in person to dine with you. Alas, he has been forced to return to his sickbed. Please, do accept our most sincere and humble apologies. You are welcome as our guest for the night.

Perceval thanked the lady for her kind words and hospitality.

While the dinner was quite good—Perceval could easily understand how the castellan had grown so fat, as the man must have employed the best cook in all of Logres—no one spoke another word. The vassals and ladies of the court of the portly lord huddled together at the other end of the hall, eyeing him warily. He saw them whisper to each other and was sure they were speaking ill of him. But as he could not hear their words, he was in no position to quiet them again with a challenge to combat.

Perceval distracted himself by staring at the tapestries hanging from the walls. These depicted merry hunting scenes, with knights and dogs chasing stags and boars through lush green woods. Perceval drank liberally from his big jug of wine and lost himself in daydreams of those serene forests.

He was only shaken from his reverie by one of the squires tapping his shoulder and telling him that it was time to retire to bed. Perceval looked around the hall and saw that the others had all left and the lamps had almost burned out. With help from the squire, he stood up again with difficulty, as his limbs were heavy from too much drink. He stumbled after the squire through empty, winding corridors until he arrived at the room he had been given for the night and collapsed upon the bed. To the sounds of hard pelting rain and the occasional thunder clap, he drifted off to sleep.

When he awoke the next morning, the sun was already high in the sky and shining harshly through the slits of the window shudders. His temples pounded terribly and, as he sat up, he vomited upon the stone floor. A servant popped his head quickly into the room, left, and returned a moment later with another one of the squires. This squire gave Perceval water to drink and a crust of dry bread to eat before leading him out of the palace into the castle courtyard. There, he helped Perceval back into his armor and brought his horse out of the stables. Perceval thanked the squire for his aid and hospitality and rode away, glad to be gone from that castle.

From then on, Perceval resolved to avoid the castles of the Logres countryside. He also kept away from the abbeys and hermitages that he passed. He reasoned that the priests and the monks were not going to be any kinder to him, but he would not be able to stop their tongues with the threat of violence. While he felt guilty about not being confessed or receiving the Eucharist, he could not bear the thought of having to sit in humble, submissive silence while a half-starved, wild-eyed monk sanctimoniously berated him because of the absurd slanders spewed about by that ugly old hag in King Arthur's pavilion.

When the weather turned harsh and he needed protection from a storm, Perceval would seize some trembling peasant by the shoulder and order him at sword point to provide shelter in his family's thatched hut. While the food was meager and stale, and the hosts were smelly and crude, at least these peasants were too ignorant or too terrified to accuse him of any dishonorable conduct. And their fires were still warm and their roofs still protected him from the rain and the wind and the lightning.

But despite his best efforts to keep to himself, Perceval eventually again came upon a fellow knight. It happened on a sunny autumn day, crisp but not cold, while he was passing through a wide meadow. Off of one side of the road, Perceval spied a rich pavilion, beside which a handsome young knight was resting his head in the lap of a beautiful maiden.

As the two of them were staring at him intently, Perceval hailed them in the name of God and King Arthur and praised the fine weather.

But the knight snapped back: By those vermillion arms, and that shield, this can only be Sir Perceval, the most shameful of knights. How can the man who cursed the poor Fisher King to suffer forever from his awful wound ride about as if he were a man of honor and chivalry? He should be covered in sackcloth and ashes, begging at the side of the road, and receiving nothing but scorn and abuse as just penance for his wicked actions.

Perceval halted. He could not let this insult go unanswered, and so he responded: My Lord, I do not believe we have met before. And I have certainly done you no wrong. If you wish to slander me, then you shall have to defend your words with your sword.

But the knight, with his soft chestnut curls still nestled between the folds of his lady's dress, replied that he had no fear of the famous Perceval of the Round Table, as God would never grant victory to such a heartless criminal over a true Christian.

Perceval now rode over to the knight and challenged him. The knight smirked and said that he would gladly take this opportunity to win glory and fame by knocking down the wretched and false Perceval with his sharp lance.

After the knight had armed himself and mounted his horse, he and Perceval rode to opposite ends of the meadow, lowered their lances, and then charged at each other as fast as their horses could go. But while the knight's flimsy lance shattered to pieces against Perceval's shield, Perceval's well-aimed spear thrust hit its mark, tearing through the arrogant fool's rib cage and out his back and sending him tumbling to the ground in a heap, pinned under his toppled horse and bleeding profusely.

Perceval dismounted and drew his sword. At the same time, the maiden rushed over to her beloved and begged mercy for his life and entreated for help in lifting the heavy horse off of his wounded body. The knight too begged for mercy with the little strength left in him.

Yet Perceval felt his rage pour over. While in the past pleas for mercy had calmed his wrath and stayed his hand, now these wheedling, womanly words only incensed him further. His quick and easy victory had proven that his cause was just in the eyes of God.

Perceval imagined this pampered young knight, crippled and embittered, spreading ever more slanders and lies as he whimpered and whinnied in a soft sickbed in his mother's castle.

With a swift stroke of his sword, Perceval severed the knight's head.

The maiden screamed. She fell to her knees, grabbed the head, cradled it in her arms, and bathed it in her tears. She cursed Perceval for murdering a helpless opponent who had begged for mercy. He was even worse, she said, than the terrible things everyone said about him.

Perceval grabbed the head from out of her arms and hurled it across the meadow. When she stood up to chase after it, he grabbed the hem of her dress and threw her to the ground. He raised his sword again and cut open her finely made gown.

She pleaded with him not to violate her and called out for the aid and protection of the Holy Virgin Mary.

But Perceval felt no desire in his loins. Filled instead with disgust for all humanity—with their endless false accusations, their relentless need to drag him down and sully his honor—he swung his sword down again; he hacked the maiden's flesh to bits, watching indifferently as her lovely rose-tinted flesh shook in its death rattle and her blood trickled out quickly through the tall grass.

V. Sin and Repentance

PERCEVAL NOW ENTERED the dead knight's pavilion, seized whatever provisions he could carry on his saddle, and rode off. He thought: Wherever he went he was attacked unjustly, as the crone's slanders had seemingly spread to every corner of Britain; not even God could defy the might of malicious gossip. He knew he should not have killed a knight who had sought mercy, much less a helpless maiden. But these insults to his honor had driven him too far into madness and despair.

Yes, madness, his thoughts continued, for otherwise he would never have been so blinded by rage as to murder a knight pleading for mercy or a defenseless maiden. A madness that had been brought on by the unjust persecutions he had endured. He was not at fault for the two deaths back on the meadow—they were not his sin—that was the doing of the spiteful old hag and all the nattering little men who whispered their mean little whispers about Sir Perceval's supposedly shameful adventure with the Fisher King. And what kind of man murmurs slanders under his breath, rather than declare his accusations openly and accept the obligation to defend them in a fair combat?

Perceval swore that he would no longer let such base, cowardly men torment him, nor did he care a whit if the Fisher King wallowed on forever in his suffering in the choking, dry wasteland. Forsaking any further attempt to find again the wasteland and the Castle Corbenic, Perceval now abandoned the paved roads of Logres and cut across the forests, riding between trees and over bushes, until he eventually reached a desolate beach with a rocky bluff overhead. Near the shore he found a faded marble building splattered with mud and overrun by weeds. It had several broad but shallow steps leading up to a portico decorated with thick rounded columns. In the center of this portico was a wooden door, which had rotted away to the point that it loudly swayed and creaked as the wind blew in from the sea.

After tying his horse to a nearby tree, Perceval kindled a fire in a pit on the ground and then lit a fallen branch as a torch. Holding this light, he mounted the steps, passed through the broken door, and entered the building. There was only one room inside. In the middle sat an altar with a marble statue of a leering man with a curly, scraggly beard and the hooves and horns of a goat. On the walls were painted scenes, in vivid but fraying colors, of other goat men playing pipes and drinking wine and chasing half-naked bashful maidens through forest paths.

At the base of the statue, Perceval was able to make out a Latin inscription. It was a dedication—a long dead Roman official, in sincerest and most humble gratitude to this goat-man god for sparing him from death in battle against some ancient British tribe or other, had erected and consecrated this temple by the sea during the reign of the Emperor Lucius Septimius Severus Pertinax Caesar Augustus, Father of the Fatherland, Pontifex Maximus, Conqueror of the Parthians.

Perceval smiled at the goat-man god. He said to him: My devotion to the Christian faith has brought me nothing but misery and sorrow. Perhaps you will bring me better luck, just like the dead Roman whom you saved so long ago.

Weary from too much wandering, and drawn to this old and mysterious heathen god, Perceval decided to remain by this temple. He rode out again from the beach until he found a couple of villages where he was able to steal the basic supplies that he needed— bedding, candles, lamps, oil, bread, rinds of cheese, even some wine. And, after returning to the temple, he found a nearby spring where he could gather water for himself and his horse.

In the course of the following weeks, he grew quite fond of the goat-man god. In dream visions, this god would assure Perceval of his divine protection and love, and of how much more pleasant life was away from all those rumor-mongering, backbiting Christians. The god would merrily regale Perceval with tales of the old Romans battling the old Britons and how the Romans celebrated their victories with orgies of wine and looting and slaughter.

One day, when he returned to the temple after felling a large stag, Perceval came across a woman sitting on the broad marble steps, with her chin resting on her palm and her face in a tight frown, seemingly lost in her unhappy thoughts. She was not young, but she was not old either. Her clothes had clearly once been elegant but were now soiled and torn. She was not pretty. She had a hard, angry look that appealed to Perceval.

She shrieked when she finally noticed him staring down at her from atop his horse. But Perceval swore that he did not intend to shame or assault her and offered her food and shelter for the night. The woman perked up at the mention of food—she was so haggard that Perceval wondered when she had last filled her belly with a fat piece of roasted meat.

With a light, warm breeze from the sea gently caressing their cheeks, they ate together that night on the temple portico. Watching her in the moonlight, Perceval mused that the woman had her charms: She had a fine head of thick brown hair falling almost to her hips and a well-rounded figure.

He asked her name and how she had come to such a remote place.

She said she would not give her true name, but he could call her Blanchefleur. She had once been the lady of a rich castle, married to a powerful knight. But her husband took ill and died from his fever. The neighboring lord, coveting her lands, then pressed her to wed him. When she refused, he laid siege to her fortress. Because so many of her late husband's knights and men at arms had abandoned her—for they said she was a fool not to marry such a powerful nobleman who could extend his protection over them all—she had been left with only a skeletal force to defend the castle. When it became clear that the situation was hopeless, she fled her stronghold through a secret underground passageway. From there, she ran as far as she could, always careful to avoid strangers and to conceal her true name, as she feared being betrayed to her pursuers.

It had been many days since she had eaten any meat, much less the fine venison that Perceval had roasted for her that evening.

Perceval said she could remain with him. He was a strong knight and well-armed. Should anyone try to seize her by force, he would run the wretch through with his sword.

Blanchefleur smiled and squeezed his hand.

And you, Sir Knight, she asked, what is your name and why are you in this desolate wilderness, sleeping beside pagan idols?

Declining to give his name, Perceval told her that he was an honest knight who had been betrayed and slandered. Fleeing the society of his treacherous fellow men, he had wandered through dense woods until he found his way to this place. While Christ was supposed to have been his savior, the Christian God had done nothing to help him—none of that famed grace and mercy and love had been bestowed upon him. But here he lived merrily and free under the protection of the goat-man god in the old temple, who had looked after so many Roman soldiers in centuries past.

Blanchefleur told how she too once prayed to the Holy Virgin Mother. Her confessor had assured her that, if only she had a true and unwavering Christian faith, God would protect her and that He was mightier than any army of knights. She had believed these words with her entire heart and devoted her every waking thought to her love of Jesus Christ and the Virgin Mary. She heard Mass each day and confessed every possible sin—if even a slight passing sinful notion materialized in her mind, she immediately confessed it to her priest in a flood of tears. She scourged her naked flesh until it bled and wore a hairshirt under her mantle.

But that devotion had not availed her hopeless cause. And now she also vowed to abandon the treacherous Christian God and to entrust her soul instead to the care of the old pagan god. Perhaps the world was more just when such gods once looked after women in distress.

Blanchefleur stayed with Perceval that night, and for many nights afterwards. They quickly became lovers, passing their days hunting, stealing, and indulging in the pleasures of the flesh. They both gave thanks to the goat-man god for protecting them from harm. They even burned bits of meat on the worn temple altar, so that the Roman god would have something to eat (or at least smell). Whenever Blanchefleur was drunk—which was as often as Perceval cared to ride out and steal a wine barrel from a village inn or an abbey—she would dance and slither over the goat-man's statue in the temple, kissing and caressing his marble flesh. Perceval, quite drunk himself, was sure that the old god was smiling and winking at him.

And thus, their lives drifted into a blissful nothing, as they did not speak of the past and made no plans for the future. So long as their bellies were full, and they could sate their lusts, they were happy enough. Later on, Perceval could not recall how long this idyll continued—at least weeks, likely months, maybe even a couple of years—it was all a merry blur.

One morning, at the hour of terce, Perceval rode out from the remote beach to a village nearby, hoping to plunder some provisions—wine, cheese, candles. But then the sky turned dark and cold rain poured down hard upon his helmet. Cursing his ill luck, Perceval made for a peasant's small hut in the middle of a field. At the sight of an armed knight with a sword hanging from his side, the old peasant couple quickly submitted to Perceval's demand to be let inside. Looking around the interior of the hut, Perceval reasoned that there was nothing worth stealing in that miserable place. He could only wait out the storm and warm his chilled bones by the fire as best he could.

While they were silent at first, the peasants' tongues soon loosened, rambling on about the local priest and about how the blacksmith had failed to fix something properly and about how someone's unwed daughter had a belly swollen with child and everyone was trying to find the damned filthy lad who had done the deed.

Perceval considered ordering them to be quiet, but then decided against it. Their idiotic babble, while grating to his ears, did nonetheless reassure him that he was happier with his Roman god and his slithering, drunken mistress than he would be entangled again in the petty affairs of ordinary men. He imagined what life must be like for the lord of a fief in the Logres countryside: Each day hordes of these gibbering peasants would descend upon you with their stupid grievances and you would be forced to listen patiently and sort it all out. And what was worse, the wealth of your estate hinged upon coaxing and prodding labor out of these fools.

But then the old peasant man said something that made Perceval sit up and pay close attention: that Sir Gawain, the famed mighty knight of the Round Table, had recently passed through their lands and stayed the night at their lord's castle. He went on at length about Gawain's exploits, killing lions and giants, outwitting sorcerers, and freeing the most beautiful maidens from captivity, who then begged desperately—but in vain—for his love and his hand in marriage.

The old peasant asked Perceval if he had ever met Gawain and if these tales were true—was Sir Gawain truly such a wondrous knight errant? Was there any better in King Arthur's court?

Perceval mumbled in response that he had never met Gawain and could say nothing about him, either for good or for ill.

The old man nodded absently and then his wife turned the conversation to her complaints about a woman in a neighboring field who had stolen her good pot, although the hag denied it, damn her, she was no good Christian and she would get a good whipping in Heaven for making off with what was not hers …

The storm eventually died down. Perceval rode away from the old peasants' hut, found a merchant caravan on the road, and easily robbed them of their wine, candles, and oil. He then turned his horse around and returned to the pagan temple by the shore.

That evening he and Blanchefleur lit the candles inside the temple and poured the merchants' superb dry red wine down their gullets. She stripped naked and danced and howled; she jumped up onto the altar and ran her fingers and tongue over the marble statue of the goat-man god.

Stepping down again, she walked slowly back towards Perceval, swaying her hips lasciviously. But before she reached him, she collapsed to the ground in a heap, urinated all over herself, and then passed out.

Perceval, though, had not been able to enjoy their revels that night. His thoughts kept returning to the old peasant's ramblings about the fame and greatness of Sir Gawain. While he insisted to himself that the world of castles and knights and royal courts was a cesspool of corruption and lies, he could not help feeling jealous of the praises heaped upon Gawain. He was a better knight than Gawain—he had knocked Gawain right off his horse more than once during a tournament. And in battles against Saxon and Irish raiders, it had been he, Perceval, who had driven the enemy away with his bold charges—and pretty, prancing blonde Gawain would always be safely behind him, like a scared little boy. He was the better knight—no, he was the *best* knight. Damn Gawain and the rest of them.

Watching Blanchefleur lying on the floor of the temple, soaked in her own stinking urine and snoring loudly in her drunken stupor, Perceval suddenly felt ashamed. He may have once been the finest knight in Camelot, but now he was a highway robber fornicating with a drunken whore who reeked of her own filthy wastes. No bard would sing his praises now; no refined and charming lady of Queen Guinevere's chamber would sigh longingly at the sight of him; and no knight would seek his aid in a difficult adventure.

The following days were wretched. Perceval no longer felt the stirrings of desire for Blanchefleur. Whenever he approached her, he imagined her naked body covered again in her own smelly piss, and he would turn away. For her part, she veered between pleading with him to remember his love for her and cursing him as an inconstant, dishonorable knight. But Perceval ignored her words; he did not care any longer if she was happy or not.

He also grew wary of his new god. What had this pagan idol brought him? Some gluttony and drunkenness, and a fallen woman who was shameless in her loathsome conduct. This god had once brought honor and glory to Roman soldiers and commanders fighting in Britain. But he had not bestowed these boons upon Perceval. Instead, the goat-man god had led him into temptation and sin, to theft, to over-indulgence, and to fornication. The marble statue of the god had winked and smirked at Perceval as he had descended further into dishonorable deeds. Perceval now understood these gestures for what they were: a demon's wily snares.

Yet Perceval still could not bring himself to leave his abode by the seashore: The prospect of once more being pelted with insults and curses about his supposed cruelty to the crippled Fisher King filled him with too great a dread.

But he also could not bear the shame of living as he had been living.

And so his soul continued in torment and indecision, until one day, when he had ridden far away from the pagan temple in search of a merchant caravan to plunder, he saw the strangest sight on the main road cutting through the fields: A long line of men and women—perhaps three dozen in all—were marching single file in identical loose-fitting brown woolen robes with no shoes on their feet. They were visibly shivering, and their teeth chattered loudly against the bitter morning cold, but they seemed to push themselves forward with a grim and steely determination.

Perceval halted his horse and watched them, mystified as to what they could be doing. When the procession reached the point where he had stopped on the side of the road, their leader, an old man with a thick beard and a noble bearing, paused in front of Perceval and spoke harshly: Sir Knight, whomever you may be, don't you know that it is a great sin to wear armor today and to ride about on your horse?

And why is that? Perceval asked.

Because it is Good Friday, the day Our Lord and Savior sacrificed Himself on the cross to redeem us all from sin and damnation. May God have mercy on your poor soul, my friend.

Then the man, with his head bowed, walked away, followed by the others in the long snaking line. As Perceval watched them go by, he suddenly remembered his Easters past. He recalled praying with Arthur and Guinevere and Gawain in St. Stephen's Church in Camelot. He saw in his mind the huge crucifix there rising above the altar, with the immense, sad, imploring eyes of the suffering Christ. Those eyes now cried out again to his soul.

He recalled once more the curses that had rained down upon him for failing to redeem the Fisher King from his torment—bitter, shameful curses, which had driven him from the company of good Christians into drunken debauchery before the idol of a heathen god. But now he wondered if maybe those curses had been God's way to prod him to atone for his misdeed and to go back again to heal the Fisher King's horrible wound? Just as Christ had to suffer His Passion, tortured and degraded and humiliated before all Jerusalem, so too perhaps God had wanted to humble Perceval through suffering and shame. And once he had returned to the wasteland and healed the Fisher King's wound, then he also could be resurrected from dishonor and scorn into glory and esteem. He could return to Camelot in triumph as the greatest hero of King Arthur's court, the faithful knight who had achieved the most marvelous adventure in all of Britain.

But, his thoughts continued, he must first return to God. He had sinned greatly and thus now had to undergo confession, contrition, and penance. Resolving to abandon both his pagan idol and his drunken mistress, Perceval rode off until he came to a small village, where he asked the way to a hermitage where he could be confessed.

After receiving directions from a friendly peasant, he traveled all through the rest of the day and into the night until he reached a modest house next to an equally modest chapel buried deep within the woods. He dismounted, tied his horse to a post, unlaced and removed his helmet, and knocked furiously at the door, moaning and howling to be let inside.

A slender, wrinkled man in a monk's cowl opened the door, rubbing his eyes and yawning. Perceval fell to the ground, grabbing the man's ankles and kissing his feet. He declared that he was a terrible sinner, a hideous, vile, disgusting wretch, and he begged the hermit to hear his confession that very instant.

The old priest awkwardly and slowly bent down and bade Perceval to rise and follow him into the chapel. There, despite the late hour, he lit a candle and urged the knight to confess his sins and unburden his soul to God.

And then out from Perceval's mouth poured a frantic confession—of his failure at the Castle Corbenic to heal the wound of the crippled Fisher King; of the murders of the knight and the maiden on the meadow; of the merchants and villagers whom he had robbed and beaten; of his depraved fornication with Blanchefleur; and of his worship of the goat-man idol of the old Romans in the abandoned temple. He spoke at such length that when the confession finally ended and the hermit urged him to rest, the sun was already rising in the sky.

For the next three months Perceval remained at the hermitage, doing penance. He fasted most days, and when he did eat, it was only the coarsest barley bread and muddy water from a nearby spring. He donned a hairshirt, prayed continually, and labored humbly in the small vegetable garden next to the hermitage. He repeatedly mortified his flesh with lashes, until he grew to savor the sticky, tingling feel of warm rivulets of fresh blood slithering down his back.

He also gave thought to the state of Blanchefleur's soul. She, too, had drifted far from God and was in dire need of confession and atonement. He pondered whether to send for her to join with him in a shared penance. But then he recalled how depraved she had been, like another Eve with the serpent—or worse, Eve with the goat-man idol. And what if she did not grasp the depth of her errors? He shuddered at the possibility that she would try to use the delights of her body to entice him back into a life of sin and filth. She was herself nothing but filth, he thought, a hungry, clawing, wine-soaked rat that could not restrain its repellent appetites. Damn her—*she* had led him far down the path of evil into sin. If he was to cleave to God again, and undergo a sincere penance, he had to leave her be—she would have to return to God of her own will, and at her own time.

Perceval never learned what became of Blanchefleur. Nor did he think upon her again.

After these three months of harsh atonement, the hermit sat Perceval down in the chapel. Sir Perceval, he said, you have confessed your sins with a full and sorrowful heart and you have undergone a sincere penance. But you were not meant for a life of prayer and contemplation. Our Father in Heaven bestowed upon you the blessings of great strength and knightly prowess. You must return to the world to complete your task.

And what is my task? Perceval asked.

Your task, the hermit responded, is the same as it has always been: to heal the Fisher King and to lift the curse from his land. You failed to achieve this act of mercy before, and you were hounded and persecuted for this failure. Those affronts to your honor kindled the wrath in your proud, vain heart and tempted you into evil and sin. If you are to return to your faith as a Christian, truly and forevermore, you must heal your soul of this bitterness—for it is this very bitterness that allowed the Devil to corrupt you. Silence the harsh tongues and mend your heart by doing that act of Christian charity and love that the world cries out for: Heal the wound of the Fisher King.

But how will I know where to find him? I came upon the wasteland once before by happenstance, but I could never find my way back there again.

The hermit smiled benevolently and put his hands on Perceval's shoulders. He spoke again in a voice full of warmth: You have confessed and you have atoned. Your faith in the One True God is restored. Trust in His Love and His Grace to show you the way.

Perceval burst into tears. When he had recovered himself, he uttered a prayer of thanksgiving, and then went to bed to rest for the night.

The next morning, Perceval rose before dawn, heard Mass, and received holy communion from the hermit one last time. Then he gathered up his arms, which had been lying in a neglected heap in a corner of the hermitage, and slowly put them back on his body. He felt uncomfortable donning his worldly gear again, and he longed to remain in the little chapel secluded in the woods, where he would be free from misfortune and temptation. He worried whether he could stay true to his newly restored Christian faith, having fallen before so far down the pit into sin. But then he remembered the hermit's admonition: Trust in God.

Perceval bid farewell to the hermit, mounted his charger, and rode off toward the nearest road, praying silently that God would show him again the mysterious and hidden path to the wasteland and the Castle Corbenic.

VI. Healing the Wound

FOR THE NEXT several weeks, Perceval rode through the forest paths and wide country highways of Logres. He spent his nights in the abbeys that he found along the way, where he shared the simple fare of the holy brothers, heard Mass, and took communion. Sometimes he would ask the learned monks if they knew the road to the Castle Corbenic, but they all replied that they did not know the place and had never been there. Indeed, none of the old and dusty maps of Britain kept in the great monastery libraries even showed a Castle Corbenic.

No one seemed to recognize him anymore, much less pelt him with abuse and insults. The monks greeted him as a humble, fellow Christian; the peasants and merchants whom he passed on the roads simply ignored him. And he continued to avoid the company of lords and knights.

Until, one day, after following a long and crooked path deep into a dense forest, far from any village or castle, Perceval came at twilight to the edge of the woods and entered a rocky, desolate landscape filled with dry, hot, nauseating fumes. Nothing was alive there—not a tree or a bush or a beast or a bird.

At last, he had found it again: the wasteland, wherein dwelled the Fisher King in the sumptuous and enchanted Castle Corbenic.

Perceval solemnly crossed himself and gave thanks and praise to his Father in Heaven for heeding his prayers and leading him back there.

He spurred his horse forward, riding hard until he reached the lake that he had seen on his first visit. Once again, he spied the boat carrying the Fisher King and his companion, and once again the Fisher King was lying flat on his back and extending his fishing rod into the water.

Perceval's heart beat fast with joy and anticipation. After unlacing and removing his helmet, he called out to the Fisher King in a loud voice: My Lord, I have returned. I give you greetings in the name of God and King Arthur. I beg the favor again of your hospitality in your fair castle. And tonight, when the grail maiden shall bring the enchanted dish before you at the feast, I shall not fail you. This time I shall ask the fateful question. Pray tell me, though, so I do not lose my way, which again is the path to the Castle Corbenic?

But the Fisher King and his companion did not answer him. Instead, they stared in silence for several long moments, appearing bewildered by his words. Finally, the Fisher King's companion spoke: Sir Knight, I give you our greetings too. But neither My Lord nor I can recall meeting you before. Still, My Lord does keep his court at Castle Corbenic and bold knights errant are always welcome to stay the evening with us. If you should deign to honor us by being our guest this night, ride over that crag—and he raised his finger to point at a particular hill looming over the side of the lake—and follow the path until you reach the castle.

Perceval was stunned. He had assumed, without reflecting much on the matter, that his previous visit had been as momentous for the Fisher King as it had been for him, and so, of course, he would be instantly recognized, and his urgent mission known and understood. But apparently, they had somehow forgotten him. And yet it could not be that so many knights had visited this wasteland that the lord of the castle struggled to remember them all. Perceval himself had never heard of the Castle Corbenic until he had stumbled upon it by chance. Indeed, when the hideous crone had addressed her grievances to King Arthur and his knights, no one seemed to have been aware of the place or its mysterious adventure.

Perceval thought surely he had been the only knight to lodge in their palace and witness the grail procession. So how could he have been forgotten? And didn't they dispatch the ugly old hag to hound him and shame him into returning to their wasteland so he could now ask the fateful question, which would heal the Fisher King's wound and redeem the land from its blight? Where else could she have come from—and who else could have told her about his prior stay at Castle Corbenic?

The Fisher King's companion called out again to Perceval: Sir Knight, I would counsel you not to linger here idly. The sun is falling quickly. You will want to cross the path over and around the crag while you and your horse still have enough light to see your way.

These words startled Perceval out of his reverie. He realized the man was right—the orange tinged, dusty clouds in the grey sky above him were dimming fast. So, Perceval thanked the man for his good counsel and rode off towards the bluff.

Once he started on it, Perceval was easily able to recall how this steep path went from his last journey through the wasteland, and he traversed it without difficulty. After he was back down on level ground on the other side of the hill, he spurred his charger towards the castle. Despite his strange reception at the lake, he was still confident that his salvation and atonement were close at hand.

When he reached the ramparts, the sentries lowered the drawbridge and several squires came running forward to help Perceval out of his armor and to stable, water, and feed his horse. But again, no one seemed to recognize him. Nevertheless, he told himself that as long as he could be seated next to the Fisher King during the grail procession, and could ask the fateful question at the right moment, the rest of their odd behavior did not matter.

Perceval was given a fine scarlet mantle and seated in the great hall, which, just as during his prior stay in this castle, soon filled with elegantly dressed men chatting among themselves. And then, with Perceval's heart racing for joy, four young servants carried the lame Fisher King on a litter into the hall and placed him down on a couch next to his guest.

The Fisher King smiled at Perceval and welcomed him.

Perceval thanked him for his gracious hospitality and praised the beauty and wealth of the Castle Corbenic and its splendid hall.

This prompted the Fisher King to speak about his castle. He recounted how his ancestors had erected it hundreds of years ago; it was even said that Joseph of Arimathea, fleeing Jerusalem in shame and sorrow because of the terrible crucifixion and torture of Our Lord and Savior Jesus Christ, had spent his last days as an honored guest at the Castle Corbenic. Each lord of the stronghold, down to himself, had added to the magnificence and luxury of its towers and walls and palace.

Perceval was tempted to ask how this barren wasteland could bring forth the extraordinary wealth displayed in the castle. But then he thought better of it: Such a question might offend his host and Perceval could lose his favor, maybe even be sent away. And how then could he achieve the adventure of asking the question and healing the wound?

So instead, he held his tongue and waited impatiently for the grail procession to begin.

A throng of servants burst into the hall, carrying platters of food and jugs of wine. Tasting the wine prompted the Fisher King to launch into a tedious explanation of the various vintages in his cellar, and how for this evening he had chosen a sweet—but not too sweet—red wine with hints in its bouquet of nuts and fruits. He had then instructed his cook to spice the wine by heating it slowly in a pot with cinnamon, honey, and nutmeg. Indeed, the Fisher King continued, he had spent many years experimenting with different combinations of spices to make just the right—no, the perfect—mulled wine.

Perceval was now ready to burst with rage. Didn't the Fisher King grasp that Perceval was here to heal his wound and restore his wasteland to bloom? Why was he jabbering on about such trivial nonsense? Was he mad? Or was he testing Perceval's resolve, trying to goad him once again into failure? Did the strange men in this strange castle even want Perceval to succeed in this adventure? But then again, why wouldn't they?

Yet then, the Fisher King suddenly fell silent, as did the others dining in the great hall. All eyes turned to a side door in a distant corner of the cavernous room. In walked a procession of five maidens in white dresses and long white veils. The two in front and the two in back carried tall tapers giving off a soft orange light. In the middle, a maiden held a wide, oval-shaped golden bowl.

Perceval's heart raced—this was the grail procession—at long last, his salvation and redemption were at hand.

The five maidens approached the Fisher King lying flat on his couch next to Perceval. After the four women holding the tapers retreated behind her, the grail maiden came forward and knelt down before the crippled Fisher King with the wondrous dish held aloft in her hands.

Taking a deep breath, Perceval shouted out: My Lord, I have a question to ask you. Whom does the grail serve?

At these words the Fisher King smiled and stood up of his own accord, seemingly restored to perfect health. The other men in the hall audibly gasped. The grail maiden stood back up and stepped back and then the five maidens together quickly and silently processed out of the hall.

But no one paid any mind to them. All eyes were fixed on the Fisher King as he walked and stretched. But despite the wonder of this miracle, none of the Fisher King's vassals or servants spoke a word. Perceval was baffled again: Why were they not asking their lord about his extraordinary recovery? And whether he still felt any pain? Or why not cheer joyously and loudly and toast his newfound health?

But far from celebrating their lord's recovery, the men in the hall seemed to have only sorrowful eyes. There were even a few scattered melancholy sighs.

The Fisher King himself, though, beamed with joy. Good Sir Knight, he said, what is your name and from what land do you hail?

My name is Perceval of Wales. I am a liegeman and knight of Arthur, King of Logres.

Sir Perceval, by your words, by the kindness and love in your heart that compelled you to ask that very question, the curse upon me has been lifted. The wound that had tormented me day and night for so many years and would not heal—could not heal—has been made whole once more by your noble and charitable Christian lips.

But still, I have not answered your question. You asked me: Whom does the grail serve? It is a simple question but without a simple answer. Please lie back on my couch—I prefer to stand now, to feel my legs finally move again—but you should rest there on the soft cushions, rejoice with me, drain the sweetly spiced wine to the last dregs. I shall tell you the truth of the marvels of the grail and of my wound, and answer your question.

Perceval's heart filled with joy. He had achieved the adventure of the grail castle. He could return, in glory, to Arthur's court, and regale all of Camelot with the tale of his exploits and his steadfast faith. He was certain to be honored and esteemed far above all the other knights of the Round Table.

He happily laid himself down on the Fisher King's couch, reclining languidly. A servant rushed over and refilled his tall cup to the brim. He drank blissfully and easily, eager to hear the Fisher King's tale and to learn the secret of all these wonders.

VII. The Fisher King's Tale

THE FISHER KING then spoke again: This was once a prosperous realm, with bountiful harvests and rich game in the forests. But my forefathers were not truly blessed until the day, long ago, when a particular stranger traveled here. He could not speak the common tongue, but he did know Latin. Still, he spoke his Latin with a kind of foreign accent that had never been heard before, at least in these lands. And he was badly weather-beaten: His skin was red and cracking, and his feet were covered in sores and blisters.

This stranger approached the gates of our Castle Corbenic begging for the most meager alms—a crust of bread, a drop of water. My ancestor took pity upon him—something about the man's bearing, something in the look of his eyes, revealed a great nobility that belied his wretched appearance.

The stranger was given a room with a fine bed and silken sheets. He was fed the best fare in this hall. Slowly, over the course of several weeks, he recovered his strength, the sores and blisters healed, and his face filled out and began to shine like the bright midday sun.

He said his name was Joseph of Arimathea. He had traveled to Britain from distant Jerusalem, where he had witnessed with his own eyes the passion and the crucifixion of Our Lord and Savior Jesus

Christ. He had been a man of wealth and rank, but because he spoke in favor of the teachings of Our Lord Jesus, he had been imprisoned by the cruel and wicked Roman governor. While he was locked away in a Roman fortress, an angel delivered unto him the grail platter, the enchanted dish you have seen tonight. Its bounty sustained him in that dungeon amidst the rats and the flies and the filth.

After he was finally released, the same angel instructed him to take the grail to the distant isle of Britain. There, he was to entrust it to a man who grasped the true nobility of his soul and demonstrated the spirit of Christian love and charity.

That man was my ancestor, then ruler of this fortress, who swore a solemn oath to safeguard the grail and use its magic only for the greater glory of God.

His task now complete, Joseph of Arimathea lay his body down on the floor in the middle of this very hall. He closed his eyes and uttered a prayer of thanksgiving full of love for God; his lips parted in a smile. And then to the wonder of all present, an angel descended upon him, gently removed his immortal soul, and departed. Once his soul had ascended to Paradise, his flesh crumbled to dust.

Filled with terror and awe of these marvels, my ancestor sent messengers to the faraway city of Jerusalem to learn more about this new faith that Joseph of Arimathea had followed. After they reached the Holy Land, these messengers were taught about the Trinity and the Resurrection and the Redemption, about God's great love and mercy and grace, from the mouths of the apostles themselves.

And when the messengers returned here to Britain, they instructed their lord and his court in the teachings of Jesus Christ. We have been pious Christians ever since, long before other Britons had learned the wisdom to reject their false idols and old gods and to embrace the truth.

Aided by the magic of the grail, the land thrived in an everlasting Spring—the fruit always ripe; fat game strolling lazily about the woods for easy spoils in the hunt; light breezes and warm nights and soft moons. Everywhere you turned, something, beast, bird, fish, bush, tree, vine, was bursting with life and beauty.

But our great wealth attracted great envy, including the envy of the so-called old gods of Britain—demons in truth, who had pretended to be heathen gods to deceive the gullible pagans. These demons were then wasting away, as they so richly deserved. With the Church spreading its light of truth across all of Britain, they were losing their libations and sacrifices and followers, leaving them frail and embittered.

But they were cunning—the Devil is always cunning.

I was a bold and impetuous youth of sixteen years when my father died, and I became lord of this castle. One evening, I rode out alone and wandered far too deeply into a strange forest. Darkness fell upon me fast. I thought I had drifted so far from my lands that I would never find my way home again; perhaps a wolf would tear me apart while I slept. In the dim moonlight peeking through the thick foliage, I dismounted, tied my horse to a tree, and sat down and wept.

But then I saw a tall maiden in a white dress walking towards me. She was holding a long taper in her hand, although her face was concealed beneath a thick veil.

Handsome knight, she said, why is your heart so heavy?

Her voice was soft and warm.

I said that I was so far from home and lost that I feared I would never find my way back again.

She told me not to worry and bade me follow her. I started to untie my horse, but she said to leave him there—she assured me he would be safe from wild beasts and thieves. I had no reason to believe her, but somehow, I trusted her anyway.

She brought me to a cave filled with a red glow, although there was no fire there and the night was dark. Once we were inside, she sat me down at a marble table and served me bread, cheese, and wine. After the meal, she lay me down to rest on a bed made of crystal.

Shortly afterwards, she joined me in that crystal bed and roused my lust with her foul arts and supple limbs. We sinned together that night, although she never once removed her veil and I never looked upon her face.

In the morning, she led me back to my charger, and, just as she had promised, he was unharmed and right where I had left him. Then she told me the way back to the Castle Corbenic. I asked her for her name, so I could thank her properly, but she had disappeared into the air.

After I returned home, I repented of my sin and swore that I would not succumb again to the temptations of the flesh. But the tall maiden in the white veil haunted my dreams, calling me back to her. When I rode through my forests, I heard the gentle murmur of her whisper in every bubbling brook and every gust of wind. I burned with a longing to see her again, to touch her again, but at the same time I was ashamed of this yearning, for I knew its source was shameful.

One restless night I could stand this torment no longer. I secretly left the castle at midnight, a torch in my hand to light the way, and rode hard and fast until I found her cave again.

The cave was once more filled with the marvelous red light.

I dismounted, tied my horse to a tree, and approached her threshold. She came out to greet me, just as before, in her thick white veil and lovely white dress. And once more, we joined our bodies together in the crystal bed and I tasted the delights of carnal sin.

And yet still, she never revealed her face from beneath the veil.

This time, though, I did not feel any contrition afterwards. The pleasures I had drunk were so exquisite that I could not bear the thought of renouncing them. And so, I abandoned my faith in Christ and His Holy Virgin Mother and gave myself wholly, in soul and in flesh, to the idols of depravity and fornication.

Every night for the next few weeks, I reveled with the mysterious lady in the cave. But she never once revealed her face to me from beneath her veil and she never once spoke her name.

One night, after my lusts had been sated, she said that she had heard rumors of the great wealth of Castle Corbenic. What was the secret of our bounty?

Without thinking, I replied: The holy grail entrusted to our safekeeping by Joseph of Arimathea.

I wish to see this grail for myself, she said. Could you show it to me?

And as she spoke, she stroked my cheek and let her golden hair, so sweetly perfumed, fall across my shoulders.

I promised to show her the grail.

When? She asked.

When would you like? I answered.

Now, tonight, she said. Untie your charger and I will ride behind you. We can reach your stronghold well before dawn.

I was nervous, though, as I did not wish to be exposed to my vassals as a fornicator and shamed for my many sins.

No doubt guessing my thoughts, she spoke again: If we reach the castle under cover of darkness, the sentries on the ramparts will not be able to tell if anyone rides behind you—there is no moon tonight and the gloom is thick. I have granted you so many favors and delights—cannot you grant me this one boon in return?

Intoxicated with lust, I agreed. Somehow my horse easily found his way through the darkness back to the castle gates and at a speed I could not fathom. He had no doubt been enchanted.

When we approached the walls, I called out to the sentries, who immediately lowered the drawbridge. We rode across fast—too fast for the sentries to come down and help me dismount—and headed straight to my palace.

Everyone there was asleep. We walked with careful, light steps until we reached my private chapel. There, on the altar, lay the holy grail. As we came near, the grail gave off a dull white light and fumes of white smoke. It shook violently and it hissed at us.

The veiled maiden ran up to the altar and seized the grail in her hands. But then she immediately dropped it and fell to the floor screaming in agony, with her hands blackened and charred horribly.

I was terrified that she would wake the whole castle, but no one else seemed to hear her.

She screeched at me with a sudden metallic hardness in her voice: Fetch me the grail dish. Pick it up, carry it to my cave.

But as the grail had broken the spell of her love, I refused.

She demanded again that I carry the grail to her cave, and again I refused.

Then she let out a howl and pounced upon me. She mounted me again as a lover, but my flesh would no longer respond to her caresses. When she realized that she had lost my love, she raised her hand, with fingernails suddenly grown as long and sharp as talons, and tore into the flesh of my upper thighs and my manhood.

And then she vanished into the air.

I could no longer move; pain coursed through my body, burning me from the inside. Sweat poured down my forehead and blinded my eyes; I cried out in agony.

My servants and vassals now awoke and came to my aid.

At that moment, on the surface of the grail dish, there appeared a large golden apple. A kindly old servant cut it into little pieces and fed them to me. As soon as I tasted the fruit, my pain eased.

But I still could not move.

And then there were worse tidings the next morning: The sky had turned grey and the air had become hot and dry. No rain would fall again on my lands. Crops failed, birds and beasts fled to other pastures, my peasants starved or left. The rich land became a rocky desert where the very air was a noxious poison.

But the grail's magic sustained this castle with its bounty.

As I could no longer ride a horse, I dispatched my knights to the demon lady's cave to discover what cruel enchantment she had wrought upon me and my land. But they could find no caves in the forest, nor had the peasants who dwelled about those woods ever seen a tall woman in a thick white veil.

I despaired, certain my torment would never end. But then one day, a stranger came to our castle. He was small and old and bent, and his grey beard was full of dirt and leaves. When he arrived at the gates, he appeared to be quite ill. I ordered that he be taken in and given a warm bed and plenty of food and drink. I ordered my physician to tend to him day and night.

When he had recovered his strength, he came to my hall to thank me. I was, of course, lying here on my couch, unable to move, crippled and wretched. In gratitude for the kindness I had shown him, this stranger offered to help me.

How, I asked, can you help me?

I cannot cure you, he said, but I can tell you how you can be healed and your land restored to its former abundance. I was once a priest of the old gods of Britain, and I know their ways. You were taken as a lover by a goddess who once reigned over this realm. However, with the Church triumphant, she no longer received offerings from her faithful, causing her to grow weak. She sought to use your enchanted grail to regain her strength.

But then you betrayed her and spurned her love. And in revenge, she smote your body and cursed your land. But if a knight, with a noble heart full of love and pity, should come to your hall and ask, without being prompted by you, whom does the grail serve, then the curse will be lifted.

When you first came here, Sir Perceval, I hoped that you would be the one to ask the fateful question and free me from my torment. When you did not, I was overcome by despair. But then you returned. I gave strict instructions that no one could tell you what had to be done. And to be sure no hint was accidentally given, we had to act as if we had never met you before.

Now you have lifted the blight that had ravaged us for so long. You ask: Whom does the grail serve? And I answer you: It serves a man with a true heart and the faith of a Christian.

Perceval was deeply moved. Tears streamed down his cheeks and he embraced the Fisher King with his trembling arms. He had followed the steadfast path of a pious Christian knight errant, bearing the world's scorn, battling temptation, and at last, on this night, he had achieved the great adventure of the Fisher King and the grail—*he* had saved the good lord of Castle Corbenic from the unspeakable suffering of a wound that could not heal; *he* had restored life and wealth to this cursed land. He imagined himself again back in Camelot, in King Arthur's great hall, telling his marvelous tale. Arthur and his knights would be in awe of Perceval's fortitude and devotion. The beautiful maidens of the court would weep and sigh, and beg to be the favorite of a knight so brave and true.

When Perceval released his embrace of the Fisher King, he suddenly noticed that the hall was silent. Looking around, he saw no one there but the two of them. This unsettled him for a moment; the Fisher King's vassals should be rejoicing, not slinking away. But then he mused that perhaps they thought their lord wished to be alone with his champion and savior; maybe they would celebrate the next morning.

Feeling tired, Perceval yawned.

Sir Perceval, the Fisher King said, it is time to rest. Go to my bed chamber and sleep in my bed tonight. I will find somewhere else to lay my head.

Perceval protested—this was too much, an abuse of such gracious hospitality, far more honor than he deserved—but the Fisher King insisted. Not wishing to upset his host, and guessing that this bed would be covered with luxurious sheets that would soothe his aching bones, Perceval at last agreed. The Fisher King led Perceval out of the hall, up a staircase, and around a hallway to a large chamber. In the middle of the room was a magnificent bed piled high with red quilts and red pillows.

As the tapers burned down in the notches on the wall, Perceval drifted off to a merry sleep.

VIII. The Wages of Compassion

PERCEVAL AWOKE THE next morning with stabbing, burning pains in his upper thighs and groin. He tried to sit up, but he could not move. Filled with terror, he called out loudly for help.

While waiting for someone to come to his aid, he looked out the window facing the bed. The sky was still a cloudy, dusty grey, just as before, and the wind carried a harsh and rancid odor. He did not understand: Had not the land been healed and restored to its bounty?

As the pain tore into his body, he started to feel feverish. Sweat poured down his forehead and into his eyes, stinging them. He tried again to move his limbs but could not; his paralyzed body shook pitiably. He called out again several times more, as loud as he could, but still heard no response. He offered up a prayer to God, but felt that his voice was becoming hoarse and weak.

At last, he heard footsteps coming down the corridor. Perceval's heart brightened—it must be the Fisher King, he thought, who would promptly summon a physician to remedy whatever strange sickness had suddenly afflicted him.

But when the door to the room opened, Perceval did not behold the Fisher King or a physician. Instead, he saw the tall maiden in the thick white veil carrying the grail platter in her hands.

She knelt down at his bedside and placed the grail on the floor. A golden apple, with a sweet and fresh scent, appeared in the middle of the dish. The maiden picked it up, retrieved a small knife from a hidden pocket, and cut the apple into slices. She then placed the apple pieces into Perceval's mouth, as if he were a tiny child.

As he ate, Perceval felt the pain and the fever subside. But when he attempted to sit up, he still could not move. He thanked the maiden, and said that while he felt better after eating the fruit, he still needed a physician to be summoned.

The maiden, however, only sighed wistfully.

Feeling confused, Perceval tried again: My Lady, please go to the lord of this castle and beseech him to fetch his physician. I cannot move my body. My illness, whatever it is, needs to be tended to.

But *you* are the lord of this castle, she replied. And you suffer from a wound that cannot be healed. You are no longer Sir Perceval of Wales, knight of the kingdom of Logres. *You* are now the Fisher King, lord of the Castle Corbenic and the wasteland.

He lied to you, foolish knight. You have not lifted the curse from this land; you have only taken it upon yourself, and freed a treacherous and evil man. By now, he has no doubt donned your fine arms and ridden your strong horse far away from here.

Permit me to tell you the true answer to your question of whom the grail serves. This land was once bountiful and rich. But its wealth was not bestowed by Joseph of Arimathea or some Christ Jesus. Those were silly childish tales meant to flatter your Christian vanity. Rather, deep inside the forest that once covered this wasteland there was a wondrous hill through which men and fairies could pass between their realms. The people of this land paid homage to the kind fairies, brought them offerings and followed their ways. In turn, the fairies brought plentiful harvests and fat game to hunt.

One day a young lord named Anfortas inherited this castle. His parents had died young, too young, and their son, just barely sprouted into a man, was not yet ready to rule. But he was their sole heir and so by right the lord of the Castle Corbenic.

The fairies invited him to their palace in the Otherworld for a great feast. There, Anfortas met a fairy maiden who was strikingly beautiful, tall and slender, with wild red hair falling to her ankles. His heart beat furiously at the sight of her and his lust became uncontrollable. However, try as he might, he could not arrange to be alone with her. The time arrived when he had to depart—for if a mortal man stays too long in the Otherworld, he becomes trapped and cannot return—and so he left with his passion still burning.

Back in his castle, Anfortas could not rest or attend to his duties properly, so smitten was he with the red-haired fairy. He tried satisfying himself with other women, buxom servant girls in his kitchens, but this only made his suffering worse. Nibbling at such meager morsels of pleasure, he yearned ever more desperately for the delights that only a divine fairy-lover can bestow.

Anfortas knew he could never have what he wanted if he had to travel to the Otherworld to court the fairy whom he desired. There, she would be surrounded by her sisters and all sorts of enchanted guardians and spirits. And if he were caught violating her, he could be imprisoned and punished in the fairy realm forevermore.

So instead, Anfortas sent a messenger to the hill where the human and fairy worlds passed between each other, and invited the red-haired fairy to his hall for a feast.

She accepted.

On the appointed night, she entered this castle, escorted by two men with goat horns and goat legs. She wore a thick white veil, because the radiance of her face would be too bright to behold in the human world. She brought the grail platter with her, as a wondrous marvel to entertain her hosts.

Anfortas poisoned the wine served to the fairy's guards, and they were discreetly removed from the hall after their bodies fell over and collapsed. At his signal, Anfortas's men exited the feast and bolted the doors, leaving him alone with the fairy maiden.

She asked him what he intended to do.

Without answering, Anfortas seized her flesh. She fought back; he climbed on top of her and tried to have her by force. Her hand then suddenly grew fingernails as long and sharp as daggers and she drove them into his upper thighs and engorged manly parts, tearing the flesh to pieces and crippling him.

She then disappeared into the air. But in her haste, she had forgotten the grail platter, which was left with Anfortas.

After that night, the fairies never appeared again in this land, and the doorway in the hill to their world vanished without a trace. The once rich land became the wasteland you have seen.

And as a final punishment, five maidens from the Otherworld—of whom I am one, which is how I know this tale—were sent to this castle to torment Anfortas, who could only look upon our loveliness but do nothing more. We became the keepers of the grail, using its magic to torment Anfortas by sustaining him in his endless agony and despair.

But Anfortas was cunning. He dispatched his vassals to scour Britain for priests and soothsayers of the old gods, whom he reasoned could reveal how to lift this terrible curse from his body and heal his flesh.

Eventually, they captured a decrepit, half-starved priest, a man weakened by years of persecution at the hands of the arrogant Christians who had overrun this island. They demanded that he tell how their Lord Anfortas could be made whole again. But the old priest refused to speak to them. Nor would he look Anfortas in the eye.

They imprisoned him in the dungeon of this castle and tortured him mercilessly, chaining him to a wall in a dark cell, forcing him to soil himself with his wastes, letting the rats feast upon his toes and the flies gnaw upon his face. After many weeks of such agony, his will was broken and he divulged the secret of how Anfortas could be healed: If a stranger, without prompting from any man or woman within these castle walls, should ask whom the grail serves and then agree to sleep the night in Anfortas's bed, that stranger would take the fairy's curse upon himself and Anfortas would be freed.

But, he added, the same enchantments of the grail that sustain the splendor of the Castle Corbenic also shroud the fortress and the wasteland in shadow, so that mortal men ordinarily cannot enter or even perceive this place. Only a stranger of great nobility and strength will be able to penetrate this mystery.

For many years, the castle awaited such a visitor. And then you came. His hopes were high, but you never asked the question. After you rode off, Anfortas set his cruel mind to work to figure out how to lure you back. His eyes fell upon the wife of one of his vassals, a vain and proud woman who bitterly resented her eternal captivity in this wasteland. He asked her to ride out to find you and shame you for not asking the question—after all, the old priest had said nothing about prompting the stranger to ask the question outside the walls of the castle. He told the woman that you would be compelled to return to Corbenic to restore your honor. And then the curse would be lifted at last.

When you saw her, she appeared old and ugly, as, being outside this palace, she was no longer maintained in her youth and beauty by the enchantment of the grail. But the ruse worked—whatever ill words she spoke to you and your fellows, they brought you back here. And after you asked the fateful question, Anfortas's deceitful tale about Joseph of Arimathea tricked you into agreeing to sleep in his bed—and thus your fate was sealed.

And so now you have taken his place. You are the Fisher King, the lord of the Castle Corbenic and the wasteland and the cripple with the horrible wound that can never heal. You have achieved the adventure of the grail and ended your quest.

When the grail maiden finished speaking, Perceval replied in a trembling voice: But why me? I am an honorable man and a good Christian knight. I confessed my sins and underwent a sincere and contrite penance. I have acted out of mercy and kindness. Why have I merited such suffering?

The grail maiden was silent for a few moments before she answered: *Why not you?*

Other Books by Barak Bassman

Elegy of the Minotaur

Repentance: A Tale of Demons in Old Jewish Poland

King Solomon and Ashmedai: A Wisdom Tale

The Twilight of the Magical Siren: A Tale of Late Antiquity

The Leper Princess and The Court Jew

The Last Confession of Joseph della Reina

The Gifts of the Fairy Melusine

Necromancy of the Demon Maiden: A Gothic Tale of Podolia

The Death of the Wizard Merlin

The Vampire and The Wandering Jew

The Emissary from Mezeritch: A Dark Hasidic Tale

The Beheading Game: An Arthurian Tale

The Holy Sinner: A Gothic Tale of the Baal Shem Tov

The Abduction of Queen Guinevere